Puffin Books

The PaW ThiNg

Oh yuck.
The mice were running up my trousers.
They wriggled under my shirt.
They were even inside my underpants.

Mice, madness and mayhem
from the magic pen of Paul Jennings.

i

Other books by Paul Jennings

Unreal!
Unbelievable!
Quirky Tails
Uncanny!
Unbearable!
Round the Twist
Unmentionable!
Undone!
Uncovered!

Illustrated Books

The Cabbage Patch Fib
(illustrated by Craig Smith)
Grandad's Gifts
(illustrated by Peter Gouldthorpe)
Round the Twist
(graphic novel with Glenn Lumsden and
David de Vries)
The Fisherman and the Theefyspray
(illustrated by Jane Tanner)
Spooner or Later and *Duck for Cover*
(both with Ted Greenwood and Terry Denton)
The Gizmo and *The Gizmo Again*
(both illustrated by Keith McEwan)
The Paul Jennings Superdiary

The Paw Thing

Paul Jennings

*Illustrated
by Keith McEwan*

PUFFIN BOOKS

Puffin Books
Penguin Books Australia Ltd
487 Maroondah Highway, PO Box 257
Ringwood, Victoria 3134, Australia
Penguin Books Ltd
Harmondsworth, Middlesex, England
Viking Penguin, A Division of Penguin Books USA Inc.
375 Hudson Street, New York, New York 10014, USA
Penguin Books Canada Limited
10 Alcorn Avenue, Toronto, Ontario, Canada M4V 3B2
Penguin Books (N.Z.) Ltd
182–190 Wairau Road, Auckland 10, New Zealand

First published by Penguin Books Australia, 1989
This edition first published 1996

10 9 8 7 6 5 4 3 2 1

Typeset in 12.5/15 Palatino by Midland Typesetters, Maryborough, Victoria
Printed by Australian Print Group, Maryborough, Victoria

National Library of Australia
Cataloguing-in-publication data:

Jennings, Paul 1943–
The paw thing.

ISBN 0 14 037770 0.

1. Cats – Juvenile fiction. I. McEwan, Keith. II. Title.

A823.3

To Bronson

1

You wouldn't read about it.

Major Mac's take-away chicken joint had a cat that couldn't catch mice. She ran after them. She jumped at them. She tried her best but the poor old thing just couldn't catch a mouse. Not one.

The cat's name was Singenpoo.

'It's the worst mouser in the world,' said Mac. 'I don't know why I keep it.' From the way he spoke it sounded as if Mac didn't like the cat at all. I felt sorry for her but I didn't say anything because it was my first day working at Major Mac's. After-school jobs were hard to find and I didn't want to get the sack.

I had never heard of a cat called Singenpoo before. I found out later how she got her name. It seems that Mac once had this tiny transistor radio. A real small one. It was about half the size of a matchbox. One day Mac changed the station after he had been cutting up fish. The cat noticed that the radio had a fishy smell and she started licking it. Before Mac could blink the cat had swallowed the whole thing.

At first Mac was mad at the cat. He shook her this way and that trying to get her to cough up the radio but nothing happened. It wouldn't come out. Then he heard something strange. Music. Music was coming out of the cat's mouth. Mac grinned. He made the cat sit on the chair with her mouth open so that he could listen to the radio. Every day after that the poor old cat had to sit next to Mac with her mouth open. Mac would listen to the footy on Saturdays. In the mornings he listened to the news at seven o'clock. On Sundays the cat was tuned in to the top forty.

Everyone thought it was really funny. Except the cat. She had to follow Mac around everywhere with her mouth open so that he could have music wherever he went.

Then one day the music stopped.

'Drat,' said Mac, giving the cat a shake. 'The battery's dead.' At that very moment he heard a faint singing noise coming from outside. He dropped the poor cat on the floor and went out the door. The music was coming from the cat's sand tray. There, in the kitty litter, was a little bit of square cat poo. The radio was in the cat poo. The cat poo was singing a song called 'Please Release Me, Let Me Go'.

Mac was cross. He picked up the
singing poo and flushed it down
the toilet.

And that's how the cat
came to be called Singenpoo.

Every night the cat ate her tea from a chipped bowl. The bowl had SINGENPOO written on the side in big letters. Not that she got much tea. Mac just didn't look after her properly. He was mad at her because she didn't play tunes any more and she couldn't catch mice. Sometimes when Mac wasn't looking I would throw a bit of fried chicken to Singenpoo. She would look up at me, almost as if she was smiling. Then she would gobble up the chicken as quickly as she could.

All Mac gave her to eat was raw chicken claws and beaks. 'It doesn't earn its keep,' said Mac. 'If it caught mice I would give it a drumstick or two. I keep it hungry. That way it might try a bit harder.'

2

On my first day Mac showed me over the front of
the shop. Out the front they had a place where the
customers queued up.

'You stand here, Scott,' said Mac. 'You take the
customer's order and then you repeat it into this
microphone. I will be out the back packing the
chicken into boxes. When I finish each one I will
push the box through this little window. You give
it to the customers and take their money.'

He took me out the back and showed me where the chickens were cooked. There were big ovens and vats for frying chickens. There was also a cool-room where the fresh batches of chickens were stored. On one of the walls was a safe with a combination lock on the front.

'Is that for the money?' I asked Mac.

'No,' he replied. He opened up the safe and took out a black book. On the cover it said:

MAJOR MAC's
SECRET FRIED CHICKEN RECIPE
of
Fifty Different Burps and Spices

'No one,' said Mac in a gruff voice, 'is allowed to touch this book. No one.' He lowered his voice and looked around. 'There are people who would pay

big money for what's in this book. Customers come from miles around for my special fried chicken. There is a new chicken place opening up on the other side of town called the Dead Rooster. If they get my secret recipe we will be out of business.' He put the book back in the safe.

'When this book is open,' he went on, 'you stay out the front. Nobody comes into the kitchen when this book is open, Scott.' Then he said something weird. Really weird. He pointed at Singenpoo. 'You stay away from the book too, cat. No one reads the secret recipe but me.' He looked at Singenpoo as if he really thought the cat could read the book.

3

Well, things went along okay for about a month. I soon got the hang of working the till and taking orders. Whenever the secret recipe book was open I stayed out of the kitchen. I didn't want Mac thinking I was trying to pinch his secret recipe.

Mac was a little bit odd but he was right about one thing. His fried chicken sure was popular. People bought it by the barrel full. They loved it. I was flat-out trying to serve the hungry crowd that turned up every night.

But poor old Singenpoo got thinner and thinner. I tried to throw her the odd chicken wing when Mac wasn't watching but that wasn't often.

'Beaks and claws,' said Mac. 'That's all it gets until it starts catching mice. There are more of them every day.'

There were, too. When I first started you would see the odd mouse out behind the rubbish bins. After a while, though, they got cheekier and cheekier. They would even run across the floor between the customers' legs. One lady screamed as a mouse ran over her shoe. She fled out of the shop screaming something about getting the health inspector.

'Useless cat,' yelled Mac. 'From now on you only get beaks. No claws. See if that will help you to run a bit faster.'

Singenpoo looked up at me with sad eyes. She was all skin and bone. She seemed to be asking me for help but there was nothing I could do. Mac was the boss. The skinnier Singenpoo got, the slower she ran. There was no way she was ever going to catch a mouse. And there were more and more of them every time I looked.

4

Then the terrible day came. The Dead Rooster opened up for the first time. They had a big ad in the local paper. They were selling their fried chicken at special low prices.

'Trying to pinch our customers,' sniffed Mac. He handed me five dollars. 'Go over and buy a bit of their chicken. Bring some back and I will see if it's any good.'

I rode my bike over to the Dead Rooster and got in the queue. I bought a Chuckit of Chicken and took it back to Mac. He opened the box and sniffed. Then he took out a chicken wing and had a small nibble. He smacked his lips and made sucking noises. He took another bite and chewed slowly with his eyes closed. I noticed that his face was slowly turning red. He opened his eyes and looked around in rage.

'It's delicious,' he screamed. 'It's the same as mine. It's my secret recipe of fifty burps and spices. They've nicked our recipe. The ratbags. The mongrels. Somebody's given them our recipe.' He glared at me with accusing eyes.

'Don't look at me,' I said, 'I didn't tell them the secret recipe. I don't want you to go broke. I would be out of a job if you did. I've never touched your book.'

Mac spoke slowly. 'You're right,' he said. He walked over to the safe and opened it. Then he took out the black book and flipped over the pages. One had been torn out. 'Ah ha,' he yelled. 'Just as I thought.' He pointed a long skinny finger at Singenpoo. 'You're the one. You're the one that gave them the recipe.'

Singenpoo crouched down in the corner. She was frightened by all the yelling.

Mac had flipped his lid. He thought the cat had torn the page out of the book with her mouth.

'Don't be silly,' I said. 'Cats can't read. She wouldn't know which page to take.'

'Look at this,' shouted Mac. He thrust the book under my nose and pointed at a smudge on the corner of the first page. 'A paw print. A paw print. The cat has been at my book.'

'So?' I said. 'Singenpoo probably jumped up on the table and stepped on the book. That doesn't mean that she read it.'

By now Mac was so angry that he was spitting as he spoke. 'I tell you, Singenpoo has been reading the recipe book. I have suspected it for weeks. One night I saw it looking at it. And not just looking at it: it turned over the page with its paw.'

I started to laugh. I just couldn't help it. The whole idea was crazy.

'Singenpoo has to go,' said Mac. 'I'm not having the mangy thing here for one more minute.' He took twenty dollars out of his wallet. 'Take it down to the vet's and have it put down.'

'Put down? What do you mean, put down? Put down where?'

'Put down. Put to sleep. Killed,' grunted Mac.

I couldn't believe it. 'She's innocent,' I said. 'Cats can't read. Someone else stole your secret recipe. It wasn't Singenpoo. Don't have her put down. Please.' I picked up the frightened cat and held her in my arms.

Mac pointed to the door. 'Even if it didn't read the book,' he said, 'it can't catch mice. It's no good to us. Go, or you are sacked.'

I took the twenty dollars and walked out of the door with Singenpoo still in my arms. She was shivering with fear. Cats can tell when something is wrong. I looked around for somewhere to hide her. There was no way that I was going to have her put to sleep.

5

Over the back fence of the chicken shop was an
empty shed. An old lady called Mrs Griggs owned
it. I knew she never went near the shed because it
was right down the bottom of her garden. She
didn't need the shed. I jumped the fence and put
Singenpoo inside.

'For goodness sake, don't start to meow,' I said.
'I'll come back every night and bring you chicken
legs and milk.' I stayed with her for about half an
hour. Then I shut the shed door and went back to
Mac's.

Mac never said anything when I went back. He didn't even ask me for the change. I think he was feeling guilty about Singenpoo.

Every night after that I crept down to the shed and fed Singenpoo on fried chicken and milk. She got fatter and fatter.

6

Things were not so good at Major Mac's Fried Chicken Shop, though. More and more mice arrived with every passing day. We had a terrible job keeping them out of sight. Mac didn't want the customers to see the mice. They were in bins and behind the fridge. At night time they slithered across the floor right in front of our eyes. We chased them around with brooms but they weren't even scared of us.

We had hundreds of mouse traps. Each morning it was my job to empty them and put the dead mice into the rubbish. Mac invented a new type of trap. He got an empty beer bottle and put a piece of cheese in the end. Then he laid the bottle on its side with the neck sticking out over the edge of the table. He smeared butter along the neck of the bottle. On the floor underneath was a bin filled with water. When the mice walked along the neck of the bottle to get the cheese they lost their footing and fell into the bin. In the mornings we would find about two hundred drowned mice in the bin. It was really bad. And it was getting worse.

One Saturday when I was serving customers at the front bench, a bald-headed man came back with his chicken roll. He had eaten about half of it. He was a pretty rude bloke because he yelled at me with his mouth full.

'I didn't order sesame seeds on my roll,' he said, waving the half-eaten roll in my face.

'We don't have sesame seeds on our rolls,' I answered.

He looked at his chicken roll carefully. Then he ran outside and spat out what he had been eating.

'Arghhhh. Arghhhh,' he yelled. 'Mouse droppings. Filthy mouse droppings on my chicken roll. You'll pay for this. I'll have this place closed down.' He ran around in circles holding his hands up to his throat.

All the customers left. Fast.

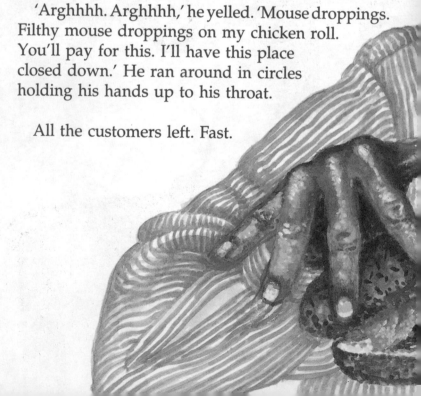

On a sign outside was written:

DROP IN

FOR A

CHICKEN ROLL

A kid who was with the bald-headed man went up to the sign and wrote on it with a texta. He put in some extra letters. Now it read:

DROPPINGS

FOR A

CHICKEN ROLL

Not long after, the health inspector arrived. He took one look at the mice running all over the floor and shelves of the kitchen and said, 'I am closing this place down. You can't serve food from a store that's infested with mice.'

He slapped a notice on the window that said:

CLOSED

Due to Mouse Plague

Then he jumped in his car and drove off.

7

Mac hung his head in his hands. 'Ruined,' he wailed. 'Ruined. We have to get rid of these mice or we'll go broke.' Then he looked at the cool-room door. 'Oh no,' he went on. 'The warning light is off. The mice must have eaten through the electricity wires. All the chickens in the cool-room will be ruined. There's eight hundred frozen chickens in that cool-room.'

He walked over and pulled open the cool-room door. There were no chickens in there. There were about ten million mice. They poured out in a great wave that was at least as high as Mac's head. We both screamed as the front of the mouse-wave hit us and knocked us over. They flooded out into the kitchen and covered the floor, the benches and even the walls. A great squirming, wriggling, squeaking river.

I could feel mice running up my trousers. They wriggled under my shirt and my singlet. They were even inside my underpants. They were chewing at my clothes. Mouse heads were sticking out of holes that they had eaten in my T-shirt. The leg of one of my jeans had disappeared altogether and the other was following it fast.

I could hear Mac shouting at the top of his voice. He was pulling mice out of his hair as he waded towards the door through the knee-high sea of rodents. They had nearly eaten his shirt clean off his back.

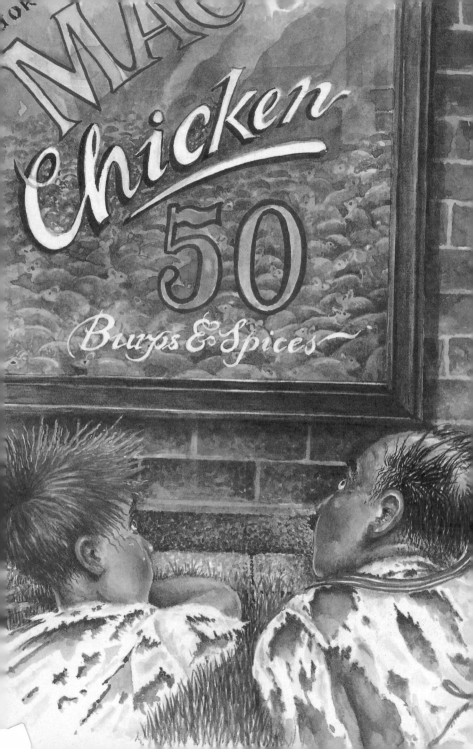

I struggled after him as quickly as I could and we both fled panting into the back of the yard. We jumped up and down, shaking out the nibbling pests and stamping on them. When we had got the last ones out we lay on the ground looking at the fried-chicken shop in disbelief. Through the windows we could see that the whole thing was crawling with mice. It was like looking at a giant jar filled with wriggling beans. I didn't know that there were that many mice in the whole world.

Just then a soft 'meow' came from over the fence.

'What was that?' asked Mac.

'It's Singenpoo,' I said.

Mac looked at me. 'How could it be?' he said, glaring at me through narrow eyes. 'Singenpoo is dead.'

'I couldn't do it, Mac,' I said. 'I just couldn't have her put to sleep. I've been hiding her in that shed.' I looked at the millions of mice. 'Even Singenpoo could catch a mouse today. I'll go and get her.'

I jumped over the fence and fetched Singenpoo from the shed. Then I took her to the back door of the chicken shop and put her down.

'Go get 'em, Singenpoo,' I said. I half expected her to run off as fast as she could go. I mean, what could one cat do against millions of mice?

The answer is: plenty.

Singenpoo walked into that chicken shop with her tail held up in the air. She gave a couple of quick, low hisses that seemed to freeze the mice. They dropped off the walls and shelves and moved away from her like a living carpet. She herded them out of the kitchen, running this way and that, darting, skipping, nipping and hissing. They seethed

out into the shop and burst onto the road.

Singenpoo stood waiting for them all to get out. It took a long time, but at last they all passed through the door. Every single one. A couple of thousand made a sudden dart and tried to get back in, but Singenpoo was too quick for them. She rounded them up and herded them back with the main mob.

Mac and I just stood there gasping. We couldn't believe it. It was incredible.

The cars in the street stopped. People ran into the shops and shut the doors. They peered out of their windows and watched as Singenpoo moved the plague of squealing mice down the main street.

Just as they reached the traffic lights the mob
divided in two groups and one lot headed off
towards the butcher's shop. I gasped. She had lost
control. In a flash Singenpoo skipped lightly over
the backs of the teeming horde and darted in and
out, driving them back with the rest. She reminded
me of a sheepdog herding sheep on a farm.

Without so much as a meow she headed the mice off towards the beach. Along the street, past the library, and down by Lake Pertobe. The herd squealed and scampered but there was no escape. Singenpoo drove them out onto the breakwater and along to the end of the pier.

They tumbled and jumbled. An endless grey waterfall of mice plunging off the end of the pier and into the sea. In the end, every last one was gone. Drowned. Dead. Done for.

'You beauty,' yelled Mac. 'You little ripper. You've saved the day. Singenpoo, the fabulous feline.' He hoisted her up onto his shoulder. The whole town was there, cheering and clapping. The crowd went crazy with joy. Especially the butcher.

A photographer from the *Standard* took photos. Everyone wanted to stroke and pat Singenpoo.

8

After a long time we got back to the shop.

'From now on,' said Mac, 'this cat has the best of everything. And the first thing I am going to do is give her a big feed. Where's her bowl?'

'In the shed,' I told him.

We climbed over the fence and went into the shed where Singenpoo had been locked up. Mac got Singenpoo's bowl and looked around the empty shed.

'What's this?' he asked. He picked up a dusty book and peered at it. The book had smudged paw marks on the pages.

'I didn't notice that there,' I said. 'It must belong to Mrs Griggs. What's it called?'

Mac turned the book over and read out the title in a whispered voice. It was called *How to Train a Sheepdog*.

A note from the author

I keep an old exercise book in my office in which I jot down ideas for stories.

A mouse plague was one idea. A story set in a take-away food shop was another. But I couldn't think of a story for either of them. Suddenly I thought to myself, 'Why not join the two ideas together?'

At that moment *The Paw Thing* came to life, but it was only in the early stages. I still didn't have a plot. Then I remembered something that happened to me a long time ago.

When I was a boy my cat became sick with distemper. My father gave me five pounds. 'Take it to the vet's,' he said. 'If he can save the cat for five pounds well and good. If not, it will have to be put down.' I walked five miles to where the vet lived. I put the cat up my jumper because it was raining. When I got there the vet told me that the cat couldn't be saved for five pounds. Naturally I was very upset. I used this little incident in *The Paw Thing* but in my story the cat lived.

The next, and most difficult bit was to try and think of an ending which would trick the reader. It took quite a while but I finally thought of something. I hope it worked on you.

A note from the illustrator

Paul Jennings, designer George Dale and I have worked together for a long time. Paul writes the words and thinks up the crazy situations. Then George and I think about how the characters would look and behave, and I turn this into pictures on the page. It's strange how it all seems like second nature now.

The 'new' *Paw Thing* was a real challenge, but I think the characters and situations are even better than the first version. And, of course, working in colour adds a lot to what has always been one of my favourite PJ books.

MORE GREAT READING FROM PUFFIN

☆ ☆

ALSO BY PAUL JENNINGS

The Cabbage Patch Fib

When an embarrassed Dad tells Chris that babies grow out of cabbages, Chris searches the vegetable garden – where he finds a baby. Being an instant father is okay for a while, but Chris soon tires of parental responsibility, until his problem is solved in an hilarious way.

Winner of the 1989 Young Australians' Best Book Award (YABBA), Victoria.
Winner of the Canberra's Own Outstanding List Award (COOL), ACT.

Round the Twist

Three short stories and the low-down on how the television series was made. Fact, fiction and fun from the fantastic pen of Paul Jennings.

The Gizmo

Some gizmos are pretty weird, but this one is the weirdest ever! And it won't go away. A wacky new story by the amazing Paul Jennings.

The Gizmo Again

It's wild!
It's weird!
It's wacky!
It's a second Gizmo yarn from Australia's master of madness!

MORE GREAT READING FROM PUFFIN

☆ ☆

Spooner or Later   with Ted Greenwood/Illustrated by Terry Denton

It's largely loopy, a touch over the top, and it'll drive you crazy. But for those who like a laugh and a challenge, *Spooner or Later* will lead you on a wonderfully wacky hunt for the Reverend Spooner's watched birds (oops . . . *botched words!*).

Duck for Cover   with Ted Greenwood/Illustrated by Terry Denton

An ingenious and hilarious riddle book with a difference. Follow the gnu as the riddles get harder! Laughs for the whole family to enjoy, from the creators of the fabulous *Spooner or Later*.

Shortlisted for the 1995 CBC Book of the Year Award – Younger Readers.

Unmentionable!

The sixth collection of weird and wonderful stories in the best-selling series which began with *Unreal!* and which later became the subject of the popular television series *Round the Twist.*

Undone!

Plans come undone. Zips come undone. Bullies come undone. And so will the readers who try to predict the endings of these eight weird and wonderful stories.

MORE GREAT READING FROM PUFFIN

☆ ☆

ALSO BY PAUL JENNINGS

Unreal!

With a literally bone-rattling start, this collection presents eight spooky
stories, each with its own twist of humour and intrigue.

Unbearable!

More wacky and outrageous stories from the entertaining Paul
Jennings.

Unbelievable!

You'll never guess what's going to happen, because these stories are
unbelievable!

Uncanny!

More twists, more laughs and more scares, and each of these spooky
tales ends with an uncanny surprise.

Quirky Tails

Eight hilarious oddball stories, each one as larrikin and bizarre as the
other, and each with a twist in the tail.

MORE GREAT READING FROM PUFFIN

☆ ☆

Beyond the Labyrinth   Gillian Rubinstein

Brenton takes his chances in a game which dangerously shadows real life, but who knows where the dice will lead him?

Winner of the 1989 CBC Book of the Year Award for Older Readers. Winner of the 1990 SA Festival Award. Shortlisted for the 1989 Alan Marshall Award.

Invasion of the Monsters   Paul J. Shaw

What do you do when monsters become real? When vampires advertise coffins on TV? Well, Ant and Cleo decide to call in Basil Kufflock, a retired monster-hunter. And what a wild, weird, wacky adventure that turns out to be!

Wally the Whiz Kid   Margaret Clark/
                        Illustrated by Bettina Guthridge

There's this kid in the class who's a real brain. Wally is super-intelligent, but he manages to get into some pretty complicated situations in this very funny Mango Street Story.

Not Again, Dad!   Thurley Fowler/Illustrated by Craig Smith

Paul knew how to manage Mum, but when she's away and Dad becomes household manager, it isn't so easy. The worst part is when Dad joins in on cricket and swimming classes – totally embarrassing!

MORE GREAT READING FROM PUFFIN

☆ ☆

Joey   Barry Dickins

This is the story of Barry's childhood and the dogs – and one special dog – in his life. Funny and poignant, with universal appeal and Barry's own special pictures.

I Hate Fridays   Rachel Flynn/Illustrated by Craig Smith

A collection of stories about characters in the classroom, about all the funny, sad and traumatic things that can happen. Hilariously illustrated by the very popular Craig Smith.

A Children's Book Council of Australia Notable Book, 1991.

Me and Mary Kangaroo   Kevin Gilbert

Aboriginal poet and playwright Kevin Gilbert tells the moving and true story of an Aboriginal boy and his love for his kangaroo.

Skating on Sand   Libby Gleeson/Illustrated by Ann James

Hannah takes her new skates on her holidays. And she makes a promise to herself: not to take them off until she can skate and skate and skate without falling over. A genuine and touching story.